Friendship Tug-of-War

Written by Erainna Winnett

Illustrated by Joyeeta Neogi

Friendship Tug-of-War
Text copyright © 2014 by Erainna Winnett
Illustrations copyright © 2014by Joyeeta Neogi

Author: Erainna Winnett
Illustrator: Joyeeta Neogi

Printed in the United States of America

Summary: Stephanie loves her two best friends, but when Stephanie learns that Emma didn't invite Claire to a sleepover, she finds herself in the middle of their fight. How will she get her friends to stop putting her in the middle of a friendship tug-of-war?

ISBN-10: 0615911773
ISBN-13: 978-0615911779

Library of Congress Cataloging-in-Publication Data
Winnett, Erainna
Friendship Tug-of-War
Library of Congress Control Number: 2013919604
www.counselingwithheart.com

To Kelly and Kim,
great friends thanks to choir practice.

Stephanie had two very best friends--Emma and Claire. She loved spending time with both of her friends. Emma could always make her laugh, and Claire always encouraged her to do her best.

All three girls were in Miss Sydney's class and took lessons together at the same gymnastics studio. It would have made sense for all three to be best friends, but there was one very big problem: Emma and Claire did not, under any circumstances, get along.

When Emma told a funny story, Claire rolled her eyes. And when Claire gushed about making a good grade on her spelling test, Emma called her a Goody Two-Shoes.

Stephanie liked both girls so much--why couldn't they just get along? It was hard to be friends with two people who didn't like each other. Someone was always getting left out, and she felt stuck in the middle.

One Thursday morning, Emma came to school with a stack of bright pink envelopes. She handed one to almost every girl in class. Stephanie opened hers with excitement and then glanced at Claire.

Claire waited as Emma made her way around the classroom,
but she never handed an invitation to her.

During recess, Stephanie found Claire crying quietly against the wall by the library.

"What's wrong?" she asked softly. Claire wiped her nose and looked up.

"You know what's wrong. I didn't get invited to Emma's sleepover! I don't know why you think she's so great, anyway. Who'd even want to go to her stupid sleepover? You should come over to my house that weekend, and we can play in my pool."

"I bet Emma just forgot your invitation. But if she didn't, then of course I'll come to your house instead."

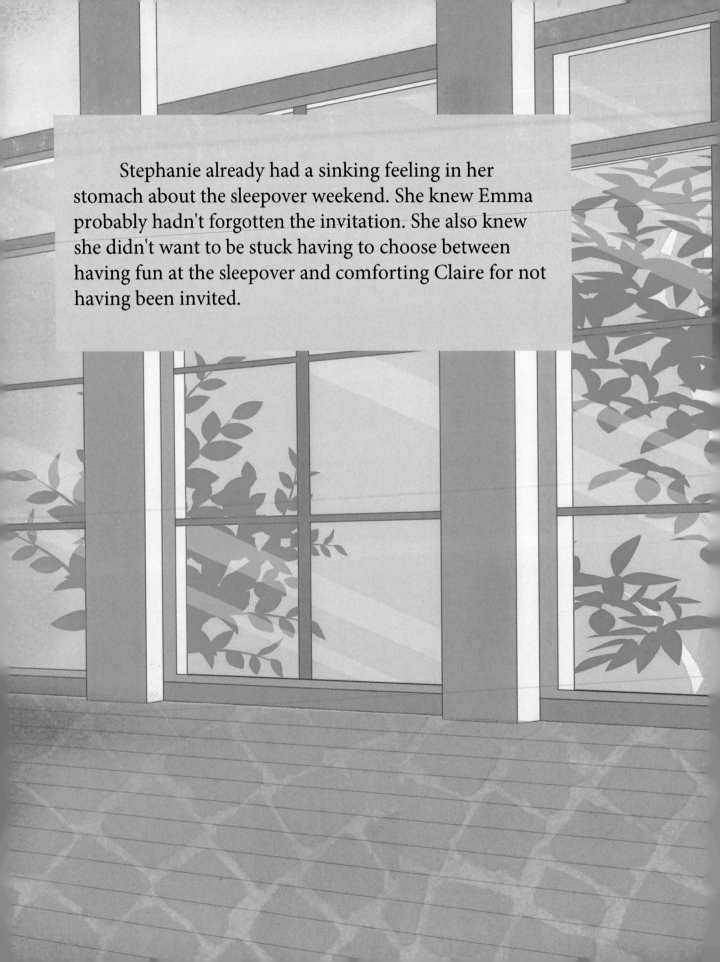

Stephanie already had a sinking feeling in her stomach about the sleepover weekend. She knew Emma probably hadn't forgotten the invitation. She also knew she didn't want to be stuck having to choose between having fun at the sleepover and comforting Claire for not having been invited.

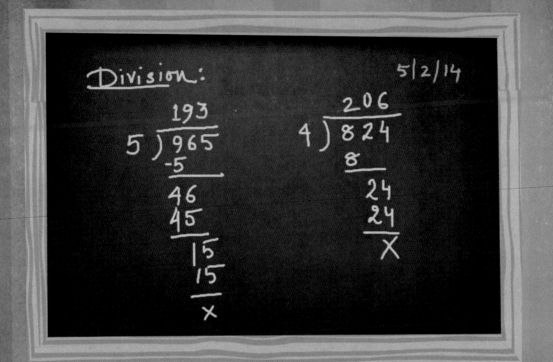

Division: 5/2/14

```
        193                    206
    5 ) 965                4 ) 824
       -5                      8
       ──                     ──
       46                     24
       45                     24
       ──                     ──
        15                     X
        15
       ──
        X
```

When the bell rang and everyone lined up to go back to class, Stephanie slipped in behind Emma.

"Where were you?" Emma whispered.

"Talking to Claire."

"Oh. Well, are you excited about my sleepover? My mom's going to order lemonade cupcakes and pizza!" Emma could hardly contain her excitement.

Stephanie swallowed her nerves. She had to ask Emma for the truth. "Hey, I think you forgot Claire's invitation. Do you want me to give it to her?"

"No. My mom said I had to limit my invitations. Sorry."

Stephanie's stomach did a double flip. She was definitely in the middle of a tug-of-war between her friends, and she didn't want to disappoint either of them. She had just promised that she'd be in two different places at the same time, and she wasn't quite sure how she could manage that.

Over the next few days, she avoided both her friends. Claire kept texting her after school, and Emma kept posting on her social networking site about the upcoming sleepover.

Stephanie realized that she was most upset about having to choose between her friends. True friends wouldn't force her to choose one over the other.

After a week of being pulled in both directions, she was ready to talk to someone about her big problem.

"Mom, can I talk to you about something? I sort of have a problem with Emma and Claire."

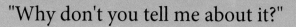

"Why don't you tell me about it?"

"Well, Emma is having a sleepover next Saturday, and she really wants me to go. But she didn't invite Claire, and Claire really doesn't want me to go. I accidentally promised them both that I'd do what they want."

"Wow, that is a problem. It doesn't sound like anyone is concerned about what you want to do." She paused. "What do YOU want to do?"

"I want to go to the sleepover, but not without Claire. I don't think it's fair that Emma didn't invite her. She invited every other girl in our class, and Claire really felt left out. But I also don't want to feel left out."

As Stephanie explained her feelings, she realized she needed to make a choice, and she knew she was going to hurt one of her friends either way.

"I think I'd better call Emma and Claire and be honest with both of them about my feelings."

First she called Claire. Her stomach did flip-flops as she dialed the number, but her flip-flops turned to frustration when she heard Claire's words.

"I'm not talking to Emma, no matter what. She didn't invite me to her party, and she obviously isn't my friend."

Stephanie hung up the phone with tears in her eyes, but there was still hope. She quickly called Emma and asked her one last time to invite Claire, but she didn't cooperate, either.

"Sorry, I told you, my mom said I had to limit my invitations."

This time Stephanie did cry. If neither of her friends was going to be fair to her, then she had to do the only thing that was fair: She had to stay home alone.

The night of the sleepover arrived. She changed into her pajamas and popped a bag of popcorn.

"Isn't tonight Emma's sleepover?" her mom asked.

Stephanie shrugged. She didn't want to talk about it.

Her mom gave her a gentle hug. "Why don't we watch a movie together?"

"Thanks Mom. I'd like that."

They had just settled on to the couch when Stephanie's phone chimed. It was a text from Emma.

Please come to the sleepover. I'll do anything if you'll come.

But Stephanie didn't believe her. If Emma was willing to do anything, she would have invited Claire.

The movie had just started when her phone chimed again. This time it was Claire:

You need to come to Emma's sleepover.
I promise, you'll be glad you did.

Now Claire wanted her to go to the sleepover? Something strange was going on. She started to call, but suddenly changed her mind.

"Mom? Do you think you could take me to Emma's sleepover after all?"

"I'd be happy to."

Stephanie quickly changed her clothes and hurried to pack her backpack. Then her mom drove her over to Emma's house. She knocked on the door and waited nervously.

When Emma opened the door, Stephanie gasped. Claire stood beside her, and both girls grinned!

"What are you doing here?" Stephanie stammered.

"When you refused to hang out with either of us, we decided we couldn't lose you. I called Claire and asked her to come to hopefully mend our friendship."

Claire grinned. "I said yes, of course."

Stephanie laughed and hugged both girls. "I'm so glad you did!"

Emma confessed, "We're really sorry we put you in this friendship tug-of-war. It wasn't fair to you and it wasn't very nice of us."

Stephanie smiled at her very best friends and took each of their arms. "I forgive you both. Now, who's ready to have some fun?"

Dealing with a Friendship Tug-of-War

A Note to Parents and Educators

There are times when, within a group of friends, not everyone gets along. Helping children learn skills to be a good friend can help them succeed well beyond their elementary school friendships. All children get upset at their friends once in a while. They may argue and disagree. This is a normal way children learn to get along with others. Its important children learn how to deal with upset or angry feelings and conflicts so that other people don't get hurt as well. It's equally important to give children the opportunity to try and work the issue out themselves. The essential aspect here is to help children understand there are many things they can do in conflict situations.

Here are a few tips to help children recognize and deal with a Friendship Tug-of-War.

• Be a good friend. If one of your friend's is hurting, it's important to be a good friend to them. They may need someone to talk to about what is bothering them.

• Maybe it was a misunderstanding. Take the time to talk to both of your friends and find out what the problem is. It is very likely that it could be a simple misunderstanding, and by talking about it the problem may be resolved.

• Avoid picking sides. While it's an easy thing to do, try and be careful not to choose one friend over the other. It's okay; you can be friends with two people. Just be sure to let each of your friend's know that you are still their friend.

• Understand. When one of your friends is hurting, take the time to really listen to them. Listen and pay attention to what they are upset about. You will be a good friend by taking time to listen and showing concern for their feelings.

• Talk to each other. These are your friends and if you are a good friend you want to let them know that you value each of their friendships. You want to be honest with them and let them know it hurts to be stuck in the middle.

 Friendship Tug of War

Sometimes friendships can get complicated. When a friend hurts your feelings, or you hurt your friend's feelings, it can be really tough to know how to respond. When two of your own close friends have a disagreement, it can be really, really tough to know how to respond. Did you know that there are some good ground rules in friendships that help keep friends together?

Have you ever had an argument with a friend? Write about it on the lines below.

_____

_____

_____

How did you and your friend resolve your argument? Write about it on the lines below.

_____

_____

_____

Were you able to keep your friendship with that person? Write about it on the lines below. Do you have any ground rules that you keep in your friendships? Describe them on the lines below.

_____

_____

_____

_____

_____

_____

Friendship Cupcakes

Write a nugget of Stephanie's mom's advice in each cupcake below. Color the cupcakes that you believe should be ground rules for friendship.

Read the following acrostic poem.
Underline the rules you think are most appropriate for
your friendships. Then, in the box, illustrate your
favorite aspect of friendship.

Freedom

Respect

Independence

Expressive

Not Needy

Dependable

Sweet

Honest

Interesting

Priceless

Each block below describes one way of handling an argument with a friend. Color the best responses in your favorite color. Color the not so great responses in your least favorite color.

Ignore your friend and give them the silent treatment.	Make sure everyone else knows the details of your disagreement.	Invite your friend to an honest, open talk about the situation.
Decide to end the friendship.	Evaluate your part of the argument and consider whether you handled things in the best way.	Ask your friend to reconsider their part of the argument and consider whether he or she handled things in the best way.
Talk to a trusted adult about the problem to get some sound advice.	Stick to the ground rules of friendship that you have developed.	Make your other friends feel guilty for staying friends with the one with whom you had the argument.
Replay the argument in your head over and over again to convince yourself that you are right and the other person is wrong.	Buy your friend a gift or write a note to apologize for your part of the argument.	Post about it on social networking, to get "advice" while secretly hoping that person will find out they hurt you by reading your status.

Now, circle the boxes that you have used in the past with friends. Cross out the ones you will not ever use with friends in the future.

In the stars below, write one quality that makes you a great friend.

Do you have any friends that you need to write an apology to?
How about a friend you would like to appreciate?
Write a letter of either apology or appreciation below.

Dear _____,

_____

_____

_____

_____

_____

_____

_____

_____

_____

_____

Your friend,

_____

Setting boundaries is a good way to keep your friendships in balance. It's important to keep yourself honest with your friends and not allow yourself to be pushed into doing things you don't want to do. It's just as important that you do the same for your friends.

Place a ⭐ by the boundaries you think are a good idea to have with friends.

_____ Pout when you don't get your way.

_____ Give a hug when your friend has had a bad day.

_____ Forgive someone who hurts your feelings.

_____ Say "I'm sorry."

_____ Hold a grudge until someone else apologizes first.

_____ Tell your friend when they hurt your feelings.

_____ Keep all your emotions bottled up.

_____ Make your friend jealous, so they'll pay more attention to you.

_____ Do what everyone else is doing, so you'll fit in.

_____ Stand up and say "NO" if you don't want to do something.

_____ Ignore the new girl; you have enough friends.

_____ Listen to your friend when they want to talk about a problem.

_____ Be understanding when your friend has to cancel an activity with you.

_____ Accept your friends' differences.

_____ Expect to spend every minute with your friends on the weekend.

When a friend doesn't respect your boundaries, it's ok to say you need a break. You can be kind to your friend without hanging around them. If you aren't respecting healthy boundaries, your friends might have to say the same to you. Practice some ways to say you need a break in each speech bubble below.

27306899R00024